The Bumblebear

Nadia Shireen

JONATHAN CAPE · LONDON

FOR NOAH, OF COURSE

THE BUMBLEBEAR
A JONATHAN CAPE BOOK
978 1 780 08015 4
Published in Great Britain
by Jonathan Cape, an imprint of
Random House Children's Publishers UK
A Penguin Random House Company

Penguin
Random House
UK

This edition published 2016
10 9 8 7 6 5 4 3 2 1

Random House Children's Publishers UK,
61—63 Uxbridge Road, London W5 5SA

www.randomhousechildrens.co.uk   www.randomhouse.co.uk
Addresses for companies within The Random House Group Limited
can be found at: www.randomhouse.co.uk/offices.htm
THE RANDOM HOUSE GROUP Limited Reg. No. 954009

A CIP catalogue record for this book is available from the British Library.
Printed in China

Penguin Random House is committed to a sustainable future for our business, our readers
and our planet. This book is made from Forest Stewardship Council® certified paper.

MIX
Paper from
responsible sources
FSC
www.fsc.org   FSC® C018179

Once there was a bear
called Norman, who loved honey.
He really, **really**, **really** loved it.

And he was always sad when it ran out.

But getting hold
of more honey
was always
a bit . . .

. . . tricky.

"If only I could be a bee," he sighed,
"I could have as much honey as I liked."

And then Norman had a quite AMAZING and BRILLIANT idea.

It was an ordinary morning
at Bee School.

"Hello, bees!" said the Queen, who was in charge. "We have a NEW bee at Bee School today."

Oʘoooh!

said the little bees.

"Everyone, say hello to . . .

. . . Norman!"

"Hullo!"
said Norman.

Ooooh!

said the little bees.

"Aren't you a bit . . . big?" asked Amelia,
who was a rather *clever* little bee.

"Um, I'm a SPECIAL bee," said Norman. "I come
from a land far, far away called . . . GIANT BEE LAND."

"Hmmm . . ." said Amelia.

But then it was time for lessons to start.

BEE SCHOOL Daily Planner

Name: Norman

They began the day

with some painting.

Then Norman joined in

with buzzing practice . . .

before everyone

settled down for a nap.

The bees showed him all sorts of games during playtime,

and Norman was brilliant at waggly dancing!

And then it was time to go home.

"Bee School is amazing!" thought Norman. He couldn't wait to come back the next day.

The next morning was even better!

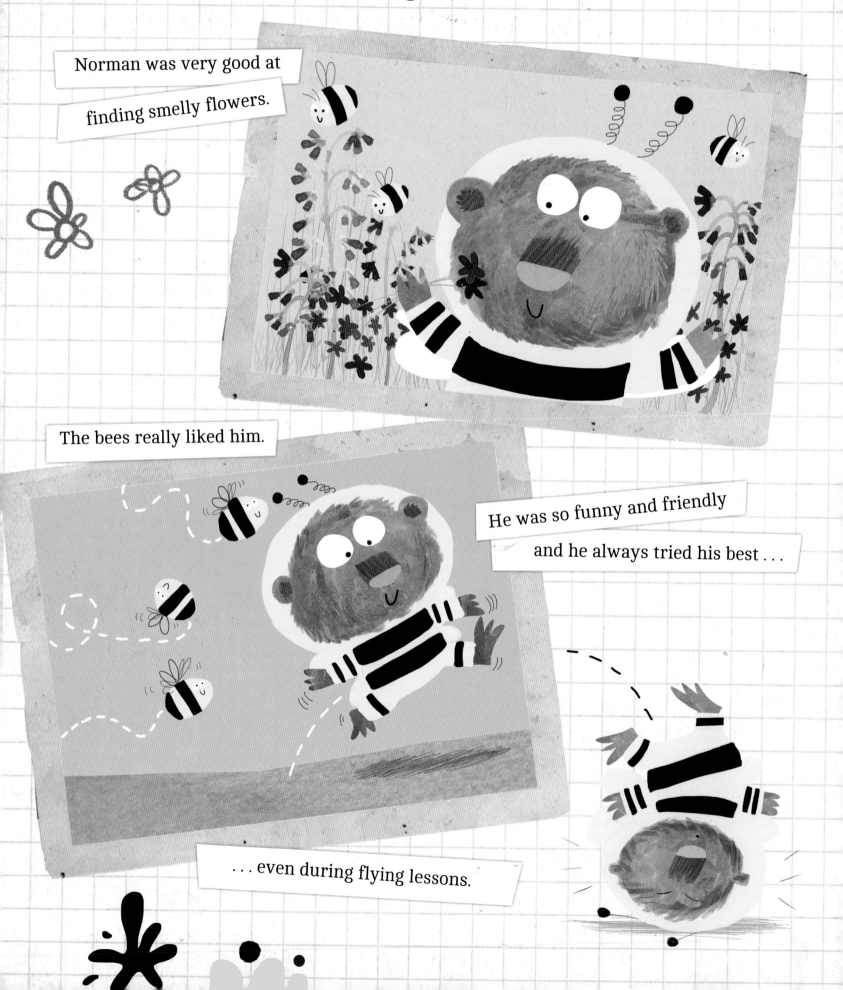

Norman was very good at finding smelly flowers.

The bees really liked him.

He was so funny and friendly and he always tried his best . . .

. . . even during flying lessons.

After lunch, the bees learned how to chase away anyone
who came after their honey, like spiders, mice, toads . . .
or **bears**.

Amelia still felt there was something
a bit *odd* about Norman. She tried to
work out what it was . . .

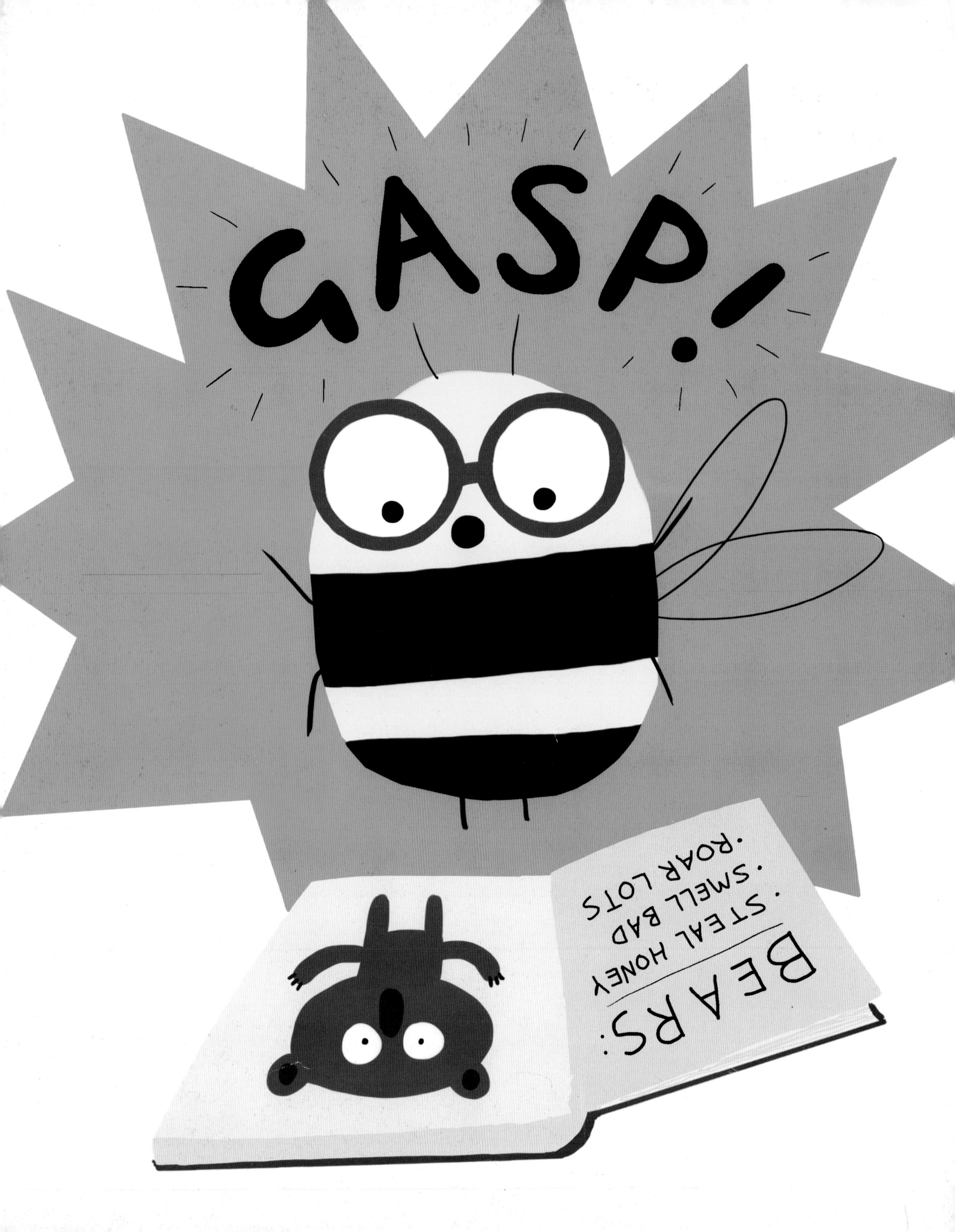
GASP!
BEARS:
· STEAL HONEY
· SMELL BAD
· ROAR LOTS

Amelia told the other bees what
she had found out, but they
didn't believe her.

"Of course Norman's a bee!"
they said. "Just look at him!"

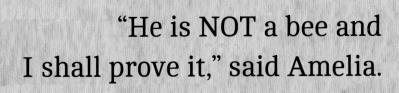

"He is NOT a bee and
I shall prove it," said Amelia.

She took Norman to the bees'

SECRET HONEY STORE

Well, when he saw
all that honey, Norman
just couldn't help himself.

After all,
he really, really, **really**
loved honey.

"See, Norman isn't a bee –
he's a BEAR!" said Amelia.

"What the jiggins?" gasped all the little bees.

"Mmph?" said Norman.

He was asked to leave
Bee School **at once**.

With Norman gone,
things were very quiet
at Bee School.

"Norman was such a
funny bee," sighed the bees.

"Norman was such a
busy bee," sighed Amelia.

"Norman was a **naughty bear**,"
said the Queen, "and Bee School
is no place for bears!"

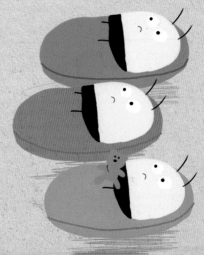

But later that night, the bees
heard a loud . . .

CRASH!

and a diabolical

ROWR!

"Oh no!"
they cried.

"IT'S A BEAR!"

And this bear was BIG and NASTY, and trampled all over Bee School. It grabbed the hive and started to SHAKE IT!

The bees tumbled out in a panic!

They tried to chase
the bear away
but it was just
too big and
too bad.

BUT
THEN . . .

...a fearsome
BUZZING
BEAST
burst through the trees.

BUZZ!

The bees were saved and
Norman was a

HERO!

HONEY

They gave him a big pot of honey, and
the Queen presented him with a special award.

"You definitely aren't a bee," said the Queen.
"But you are no ordinary bear. You are, I think –
a BUMBLEBEAR."

And bumblebears were definitely allowed to go back to

BEE SCHOOL!

THE END